This book

_____

Contents

Cover illustration by Guy Parker-Rees
Text pages 15-18 by Judith Nicholls (© MCMXCVII)

Published by Ladybird Books Ltd
80 Strand London WC2R 0RL
A Penguin Company
8 10 9

ISBN-13: 978-0-72142-390-6
Printed in China

What's that noise?

written by Geraldine Taylor

illustrated by Guy Parker-Rees

Kim and her family
were camping.
That night, Kim and her
dad couldn't sleep.
Mum was snoring!

4

Dad whispered, "It's much too noisy in here. Let's go out for a quiet walk."

5

Kim and Dad got dressed and
went outside.

"What was that?"
whispered Kim.
"Don't worry," said Dad.
"It's only an owl."

9

"What was that?" asked Kim.
Dad said, "Don't worry.
It's only a dog."

Kim and her dad nearly fell
over in surprise.
"What was that?" asked Dad.

"It was only that sheep over there," said Kim.
"Is it time to go back?"

Tyrannosaurus rex

written by Judith Nicholls

illustrated by Andy DaVolls

I am the **biggest** dinosaur.
My neck is as tall as a tree.
I am **Tyrannosaurus rex**.
Don't touch **me**!

I am the **biggest** dinosaur.
My body's as big as a lorry.
I am **Tyrannosaurus rex**.
If you touch me you'll be **sorry**.

I am the **biggest** dinosaur.
My tail is as strong as a train.
I am **Tyrannosaurus rex**.
I am the **King** of the Plain.

The last dinosaur

written by Marie Birkinshaw

illustrated by Rosslyn Moran

Sam Brown's bedroom was full of dinosaurs. It was also very untidy.

Sam Brown loved collecting
things about dinosaurs,
but he never had time
to put them away.

Now Sam was collecting
dinosaur cards, and he
needed just one more card
for a full set.

The card he needed was
a Giganotosaurus, one of
the last dinosaurs ever
to be found.

He had asked all his friends
at school, but nobody had
the Giganotosaurus.

He asked his mum if he could go out to get some more cards. But Mum said no. She said he had to tidy up his bedroom.

Sam didn't want to.
Tidying up was really boring.

But then Sam began to like
it. He found some dinosaurs
that he hadn't looked at
for a long time.

Suddenly he saw something
under his bed.

It was a pack of dinosaur cards
that he hadn't opened.

Sam quickly looked inside.

There was a Stegosaurus,
an Apatosaurus and...

a GIGANOTOSAURUS!

At last! Sam had the full set.
Tidying up wasn't so bad,
after all.

Dinosaur Facts

- We know of about 250 different kinds of dinosaurs. There are probably hundreds of different types that have yet to be discovered.

- Dinosaurs existed for 160 million years – a long time compared with the mere two million years or so that humans have been on Earth.

- Tyrannosaurus rex existed 70 million years ago. It was once thought to be the biggest meat-eating dinosaur. Recent discoveries have unearthed an older dinosaur that dwarfed Tyrannosaurus rex. The Giganotosaurus existed 100 million years ago. It weighed between six and eight tonnes and measured 12.5 metres long. It had a huge head, massive jaws and lots of sharp teeth.

- Dinosaurs were probably brightly coloured. Even the drab dinosaurs may have had bright frills and crests.

- The biggest dinosaurs were the long-necked plant-eaters. The biggest was Seismosaurus. It must have weighed 100 tonnes – equal to fifteen elephants.

- The biggest dinosaur footprints discovered so far are over one metre in diameter. They were found in Argentina, in South America.

- The meat-eating dinosaurs used to prey on the plant-eating dinosaurs. So the plant-eaters needed plenty of armour to defend themselves. Some developed spines on their backs and sides and even had clubs on their tails.

- One of the biggest plated dinosaurs was the Stegosaurus. It was seven metres long and lived in North America.

My funnybone's not funny

written by Geraldine Taylor

illustrated by Tania Hurt-Newton

My funny bone's
not funny.

And my big toe's
much too big.

My knees are
wobbly knobbly.

And my leg looks
like a twig.

I wish I could run faster.
I wish I could climb a tree.

I wish I could be lots of things.
But I'm really glad I'm **me!**